JUST LIKE DADDY

Grosset & Dunlap

For *my* daddy, with love — M.E.B.

Love & sweet kisses to my boys, Jack & Rick — S.P.

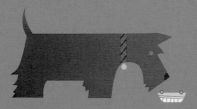

Text copyright © 2003 by Megan E. Bryant. Illustrations copyright © 2003 by Stacy Peterson.
All rights reserved. Published by Grosset & Dunlap, a division of Penguin Young Readers
Group, 345 Hudson Street, New York, NY, 10014. GROSSET & DUNLAP is a trademark of
Penguin Group (USA) Inc. Published simultaneously in Canada. Manufactured in China.

Library of Congress Cataloging-in-Publication Data

Bryant, Megan E.
    Just like daddy / by Megan E. Bryant ; illustrated by Stacy Peterson.
        p. cm.
    Summary: Rhyming text and illustrations show ways in which some fathers
and sons are alike.
    [1. Fathers--Fiction. 2. Stories in rhyme.] I. Peterson, Stacy, ill. II. Title.
PZ8.3.B835 Jt 2003
[E]--dc21

                                                            2002151248

ISBN 0-448-43106-8   B C D E F G H I J

JUST LIKE DADDY

By Megan E. Bryant

Illustrated by Stacy Peterson

Grosset & Dunlap • New York

Daddy was a lot like you
when he was just a kid —
today, you do a lot of things
that once your daddy did!

Playing games, doing homework,
watching TV, too —
it's fun to see all the ways
your daddy was like you!

You go on family vacations . . .

just like Daddy.

You love to play in water when it's hot . . .

just like Daddy.

You ride the biggest, scariest, fastest roller coasters . . .

just like Daddy.

You play awesome games . . .

just like Daddy.

You wear cool sneakers . . .

just like Daddy.

You ride fast on your scooter . . .

just like Daddy.

You help clean your room . . .

You don't like getting dressed up . . .

Cheddar Chips

Salsa

Lunch Snacks
Tacos

just like Daddy.

You have a really cool toy car . . .

just like Daddy.

You love listening
to music . . .

just like Daddy.

Daddy's all grown up now, but once he was like you —
he used to be a little boy who loved his daddy, too.
Every day you're growing up,
and changing as you grow.
And Daddy will always love you —
more than you'll ever know.